we will ROCK our
CLASSMATES

#1 *NEW YORK TIMES* BEST-SELLING AUTHOR

RYAN T. HIGGINS

Los Angeles   New York

For Paul

I would like to thank the kids who made the artwork for the endpapers: Billy, Cece, Charlie, Cora, Eben, Eliana, Ethan, Evelyn, Evie, Grant, Griffin, Jack, Jillian, Karen, Luna, Noah, Teddy, and Vivian.

I also need to thank two grown-up kids, Joanna and Annie, who helped make this book.

First Edition, July 2020
10 9 8 7 6 5 4 3 2
FAC-029191-20173
Printed in Malaysia

This book is set in Macarons/Fontspring with hand-lettering by Ryan T. Higgins
Designed by Tyler Nevins
Illustrations were created using scans of treated clayboard for textures, graphite, ink, and Photoshop

Library of Congress Cataloging-in-Publication Data

Names: Higgins, Ryan T., author, illustrator.
Title: We will rock our classmates / Ryan T. Higgins.
Description: First edition. • Los Angeles : Disney–Hyperion, 2020. •
    Audience: Ages 3–5. • Summary: As the only T. rex in her school,
    Penelope is often overlooked, but when she loses her confidence after
    signing up for the school talent show, her father and some friends help
    her find her courage.
Identifiers: LCCN 2019044013 • ISBN 9781368059596 (hardcover)
Subjects: CYAC: Tyrannosaurus rex—Fiction. • Dinosaurs—Fiction. • Talent
    shows—Fiction. • Self-confidence—Fiction. • Schools—Fiction. •
    Humorous stories.
Classification: LCC PZ7.H534962 Wg 2020 • DDC [E]—dc23
LC record available at https://lccn.loc.gov/2019044013

Reinforced binding
Visit www.DisneyBooks.com

Penelope was the only T. rex in her school.

H. Mitchell School
Mrs. Noodleman Kindergarten

Sometimes that made her stand out a little.

And sometimes Penelope's classmates didn't see her at all.
They just saw a dinosaur.

Dinosaur or not,
Penelope loved to play.

She loved to read.

But the one thing Penelope loved to do
    more than anything else was to make music.

She loved to sing.

She loved to play guitar.

Penelope loved
to rock 'n' roll.

So when Mrs. Noodleman told the class about the school talent show, Penelope was excited.

She was also nervous.

She wanted to rock
her classmates.
But could she do it?

Also, the sign-up sheet was right next to Walter the ferocious goldfish.

Penelope took a deep breath.

She had to do it.

She tiptoed past Walter.

Then she quickly wrote her name with her bravest purple marker.

After school, Penelope shared the big news with her parents.

She hummed her favorite songs while brushing her teeth.

She danced all the way to the bus.

She even told her classmates about her favorite band, the Weevils.

Best. Band. Ever. My dad used to go to all their concerts . . .

until he accidentally ate the drummer.

At last, it was time
for the rehearsal.

Onstage,
Penelope froze.

She could not sing.

She could NOT play guitar.

She worried that . . .

dinosaurs could not rock 'n' roll.

Penelope was very quiet on the car ride home.

She hardly ate anything for supper.

Are you sure you don't want more, Penny Pie? You've only had 52 burgers.

The next day at recess, Penelope sat alone on the bench.

She would not play hopscotch.

I am a T. rex, not a hopscotcher.

She would not play duck, duck, goose.

I am not a duck or another duck or a goose.

I am a dinosaur.

At the end of the day,
Penelope crossed her name
off the sign-up sheet
with her saddest blue marker.

When Penelope got home,
she went straight to her room.

Daddy Rex came in to talk to her.
"Is everything okay?" he asked.

"I can't be in the talent show,"
she cried. "I am just a dinosaur."

"Ah, I see," said Daddy Rex.
"Come with me."

Take a look at this family photo album.
This is your uncle Frank. He was a figure skater.
Oh, and here's your mom finishing her first marathon.
07

And here's me, the world hamburger-eating champion. I ate 5,053 hamburgers . . . with ketchup!

"You see?" said Daddy Rex.
"Being a T. rex is only part of who you are.
You, for instance, are kind and caring,
creative and adventurous,
AND you can be anything you want to be."

The next day at school,
Penelope marched back over
to the sign-up sheet.

She looked straight at Walter
and almost lost her nerve.

Talent Show
Sign-up Sheet

Name	talent
~~Penelope~~	~~Rock Mull~~
Will	SOUNDS
MABEL	DANCE
Stegmans	MIME
Martina	Magic

But Penelope's classmates had a different idea.

And that gave her just enough courage.

On the night of the show, Penelope was really excited and also really nervous.

She peeked out from backstage to try and find her parents.

When the curtains opened, William Omoto and his amazing animal sounds took the stage.

Mabel Haystings and her dancing pony went second.

Then there was the Stegman Brothers' synchronized swimming mimes act . . .

followed by Martina Cortez and her dazzling card tricks.

Finally, it was Penelope's turn.

The lights on the stage were bright,
but not as bright as Penelope.

We are . . . Penelope and
the Mustard Seeds!

Penelope was a T. rex.
She was also kind and caring
and creative and adventurous.

Most of all . . .

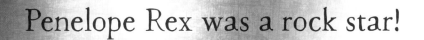

Penelope Rex was a rock star!

Penelope and the Mustard Seeds came in second place, just behind Mabel Haystings and her dancing pony.

That was okay with Penelope.
She loved ponies.

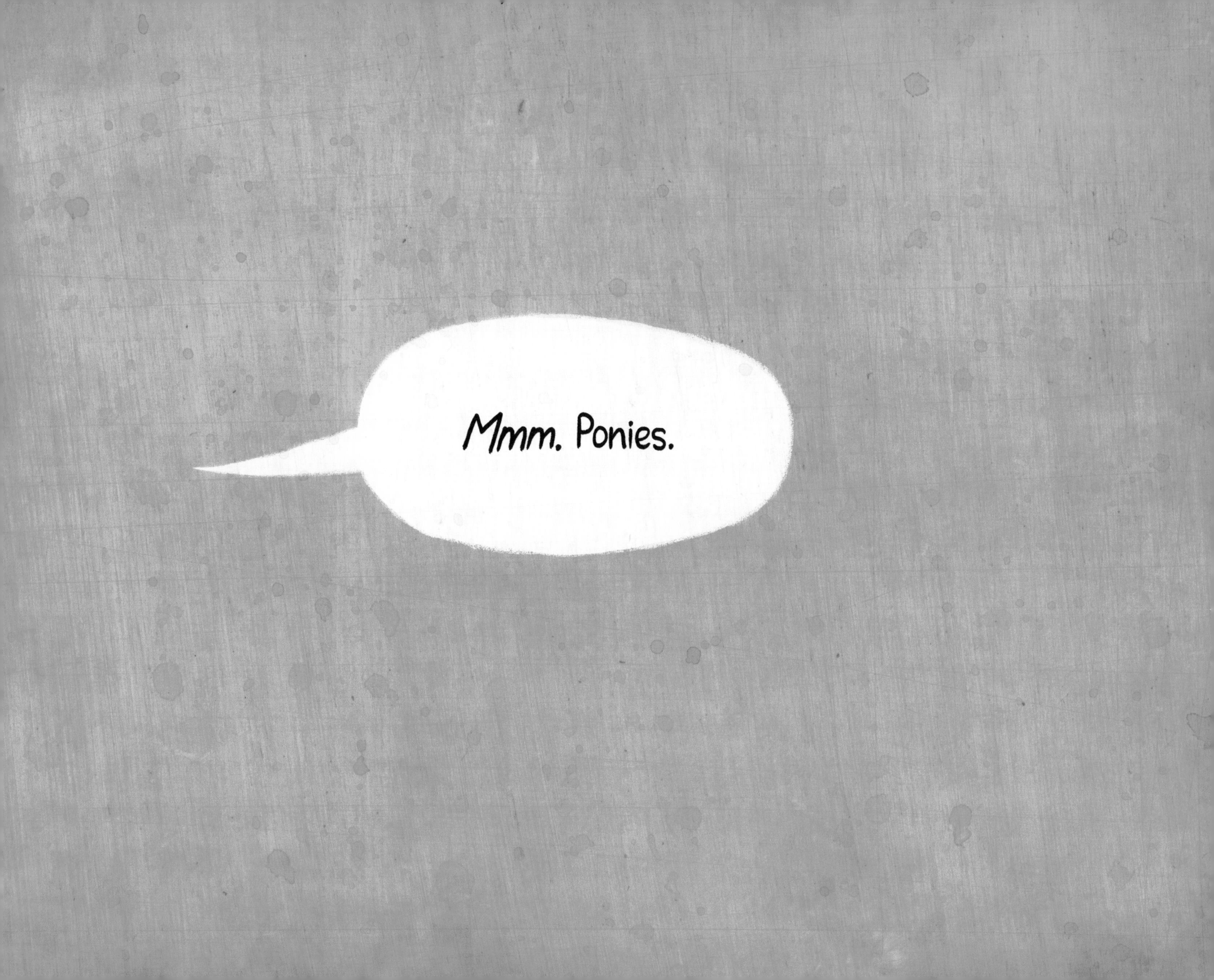
Mmm. Ponies.